THE CHRIST

Wendy Douthwaite lives with her husband near Bristol, where they run a bookselling business. She has written a number of pony stories, including *The Orange Pony* and the Polly series.

THE CHRISTMAS PONY

Wendy Douthwaite

MACMILLAN
CHILDREN'S BOOKS

First published 1985 by Blackie and Son Limited

This edition published 1996 by Macmillan Children's Books
a division of Macmillan Publishers Limited
25 Eccleston Place, London SW1W 9NF
and Basingstoke

Associated companies throughout the world

ISBN 0 330 34700 4

1 3 5 7 9 8 6 4 2

A CIP catalogue record for this book is available from
the British Library.

Phototypeset by Intype London Ltd
Printed by Mackays of Chatham plc, Kent

Contents

I Really Will Try

She would be in there!

Lindy stopped and looked towards home. Late leaves of autumn danced in crazy circles across the lane, driven by a biting December wind. Lindy shivered and continued on her way, hurrying through the cobbled entrance yard of Court Farm.

From the kitchen window, a thin finger of light stretched welcomingly across the little square of lawn, lighting the way to the front door. Lindy raised the latch and let herself into the cold, stone-flagged hall.

"That you, Lindy?"

Her father's voice came from the kitchen, as did the light which dimly lit the hall from the half open kitchen door.

Lindy opened her mouth to answer, but then she remembered, and coldness crept around her heart. She turned away from the welcoming warmth of the kitchen and moved towards the stairs.

"Linda!"

She turned back, recognising a sharpness in her father's tone. There would be more trouble if she did not answer.

"Yes," she replied, flatly.

Mr Cottham looked up as Lindy appeared in the doorway.

"Come on, love," he said, more gently this time. "We've been waiting for you." He looked across the room at the thin eleven-year-old who gazed back at him guardedly from brown eyes which were so like his own.

"She's the spitting image of you," Lindy's mother had been fond of saying. "Just like peas in a pod, you two are!"

But now Lindy's mother was dead, and there stood Lindy, pale and defiant. Mr Cottham sighed, remembering how close he and Lindy had become after his wife died. But now . . .

"Shut the door, Lindy, and keep the warmth in, will you? We're all in now." Lindy glided round the back of his chair to her favourite place, the inglenook of the huge, farmhouse range, which sent out a glow of warmth and light through its metal bars.

Jim, Lindy's older brother, grunted a greeting before leaning over to switch on the radio.

As the friendly burr of sound from the old radio floated around her, Lindy sat in her place, noticing her father's worried expression; seeing the tiredness in his eyes.

Tonight, I really *will* try, she promised herself. Her eyes wandered across to the big, oak table, where chrysanthemums glowed against the dark wood. I *must* try, she told herself again. I *won't* be rude to Susan.

Susan's face appeared round the scullery door, and she smiled in Lindy's direction. Lindy tried to return the smile, studying her for a moment and wondering *why*. Why did she feel so full of resentment, when Susan tried so hard to be friendly? Lindy turned her face away from Susan's gaze, and stared into the fire, continuing the questions in her mind.

Why couldn't we have stayed the way we were, she wondered, bitterly. It had been horrible without Mum – an empty void which nothing seemed to fill. But they had been together, just the three of them – Dad, Jim and her. And it had worked all right. Lindy kicked at the old metal fender, angrily. Why did Dad have to go off and marry Susan, just as they were all settling down? Susan was too young for him, anyway – not much more than thirty, Lindy thought. It had all happened so quickly, too.

Dad had met Susan at a farming conference, and had only known her for two months when he invited her down from the North, where she lived, to stay for the weekend. It had been a disastrous weekend, from Lindy's point of view. Dad had taken Susan out every night, and Lindy had sat sullenly at home with Jim, jealous of all the attention that Susan was having from the parent who had been mother and father to her for the past two years.

Then Dad had announced his intention to marry Susan.

"You *do* understand, don't you, Lindy?" Dad had asked. "I'm not very good at explaining these things. You know I loved Mum – we all did. But . . . life has to go on . . . and Susan and I get on so well. I'm sure you'll like her, too, when you get to know her. She so much wants to be a mother to you."

Mr Cottham could not have chosen worse words. Lindy's hackles had risen at the thought of this interloper trying to take her mother's place, and Susan, when she had arrived at the farm after the honeymoon, had come up against a hostile and unyielding eleven-year-old, who retreated to her bedroom at every opportunity.

"Would you like one?"

Lindy looked up suddenly to see Susan looking towards her. She was bending down now, in front of the range, taking a dish of baked potatoes from the lower oven. Her brown, shoulder-length hair fell across her face; a happy kind of face, Lindy was bound to admit, with clear, grey eyes which were both friendly and guarded as they looked into hers.

"I'm not hungry," Lindy lied, staring at the potatoes, sullenly.

"Linda," Dad said, sharply, pausing to glare at his daughter. "Take a potato and stop messing."

Lindy opened her mouth to retort, but Jim saved the situation for the moment. He leaned over, picked up the biggest potato and broke it in half.

"Share it with me," he said, winking at her, and his cheery face melted away her anger.

After supper, silence descended on the room. Having listened to the news, Dad had turned off the radio, and the only sounds were the ticking of the grandfather clock in the corner and the occasional hiss and crackle of the fire in the grate.

Dad broke the silence.

"I thought I might go to Yatebury Market next Wednesday," he said.

Excitement lurched in Lindy's stomach and she looked up quickly. But Dad was looking in Susan's direction as he said, "Do you think you'd like to go with me, love?"

Aware of Lindy's watchful eyes, Susan thought for a moment.

"I'd like to, of course," she said, slowly, "but I think I'd better get on with the Christmas things next week." She looked at her step-daughter. "Lindy, perhaps *you'd* like to go with Dad?"

"But you'll still be at school, won't you, Lindy?" Dad asked.

Lindy hesitated. "Well, yes, but . . ." she agreed, slowly. She hesitated again. Somehow, she seemed to be on the wrong side of this discussion – Susan's side.

"But Doug, they don't do much school work at this time of year," Susan broke in. "It's mostly rehearsals for the Christmas play next week, isn't it, Lindy?"

6

Lindy nodded, desperately torn between her resentment of Susan and her desire to visit Yatebury Market.

At last, Dad realised what Susan was trying to do. "Well, all right then, Lindy, love. If Susan doesn't want to come, then I'll have a word with Miss Matthews at school and see if you can have a day off. Would you like that?" Lindy grudgingly mumbled her agreement.

"Well, that's settled, then." Susan looked across the table at Lindy. Lindy looked back, moodily, half wishing that she had declined the offer. Susan seemed to think that persuading Dad to take her to Yatebury Market had somehow brought the two of them together.

Well, thought Lindy, angrily, twisting the hanging fringe of the check tablecloth round and round in her fingers, she needn't think she can take Mum's place by getting round me.

Her mind drifted away from these uncomfortable thoughts towards Yatebury Market.

Lindy pushed her chair back from the table. "Can I go now, please?" she asked.

Dad grinned. "Off you go, then," he said.

CHAPTER TWO

The Pony Fund

Thankfully, Lindy closed her bedroom door behind her. She hurried across to the chest of drawers and pulled open the bottom drawer. Carefully lifting out a small cash box, she carried it over to her bed.

Sitting cross-legged on her bed, Lindy tugged impatiently at the thin cord around her neck and pulled it out from under her shirt. On the end of the cord was a small key, which she used to open the cash box.

Inside the box, on top of a pile of notes and some change, was a small, well-worn notebook and a much-chewed pencil.

Suddenly Lindy remembered Mrs Tucker. Unfolding her legs from beneath her, she crossed over to the door where she had hung her duffle coat. Rummaging around in the pocket, she pulled out three twenty-pence pieces. As she took them back to her bed, Lindy thought about old Mrs Tucker, who had been a good friend to her, helping her through the terrible time when her mother had died.

Mrs Tucker was a widow who lived just across the lane from Court Farm, in Number Three, Hillside Cottages. She was badly crippled with arthritis, but managed to live an independent life with the help of her only son and his wife, who lived a quarter of a mile away. Her neighbours helped as well, and Lindy called in at the cottage every day after school, to do any little odd jobs and to talk to her.

Mrs Tucker hated the twenty-pence pieces which regularly arrived in her change when her groceries were delivered.

"You have them, dear," she said, when they appeared in her purse. "I hate the silly little things – they look too much like the ten-pence pieces for my liking. You put them towards that little pony you're going to buy, one day."

"But Mrs Tucker," Lindy said, as she put more coal on the fire, "they're worth a lot more than the ten-pence pieces –

you only need five of them to make a pound."

"Look, my dear," Mrs Tucker replied, leaning forward in her chair, the firelight flickering on her old lined face. "I don't like them. They worry me, and I don't have so very many – only one or two a week, usually." She looked up at the wall, smiling. "Besides," she continued, "you know that *I* love horses, too."

Following her gaze, Lindy looked again at the faded old photograph which hung on the wall. Two huge carthorses stood patiently, harnessed to a long cart, to which was chained a pile of tree-trunks. Beside the cart, dwarfed by its size, was a small governess cart, drawn by a pony. It was difficult to believe that the girl sitting primly on one of the seats, dressed in a high-necked dress and long, buttoned boots, was old Mrs Tucker. Holding the reins was her older brother, and standing beside the two carthorses was Mrs Tucker's father, his mutton-chop whiskers and moustache seeming to bristle with pride.

"Oh yes, they were such lovely days." How often Lindy had heard old Mrs Tucker say those words, with a sigh, and how often Lindy had tried to imagine lame old Mrs Tucker running with her hoop and stick, or climbing all around and under those patient carthorses as they stood in their stables.

"Tell me again about the horses," Lindy urged. "The one on this side was Bob and the other one with the wicked gleam in his eye – that was Boxer, wasn't it?"

Mrs Tucker nodded. "And then there was Gypsy – the little brown pony, there."

"Oh yes." Lindy sat down by the hearth and drew her knees up under her chin. "Little Gypsy was clever, wasn't she – and naughty."

Mrs Tucker chuckled and began again to tell the stories which Lindy had heard many times before and which were now lodged firmly in her mind – stories of days and times which she could hardly comprehend. Days when horses were prized and loved; slower days.

This was how Lindy spent much of her time with Mrs Tucker, now that winter was here. On summer evenings, with old Mrs Tucker leaning heavily on Lindy's arm on one side and on her stick on the other, they had wandered out into the little pocket-handkerchief garden to sit under the apple tree, where Mrs Tucker would tell tales of Sunday School outings and family stories.

Lindy's thoughts about Mrs Tucker were interrupted by a rattle at the bedroom window and a thin cry. She pulled back the curtain. On the sill outside sat a young tabby cat, his green eyes blinking in the light which spilled out from the bedroom window.

Unlatching the window, Lindy opened it a few inches, letting in a cold blast of air as well as the tabby cat, who slipped quickly in through the gap.

Lindy shivered. "It's cold out there, Pinky, isn't it, little puss," she crooned. The tabby purred loudly and rubbed against Lindy's arm. Lindy closed the latch tightly.

Gathering Pinky up into her arms, Lindy carried him over to her bed. His tabby fur smelled of frost and fresh air and his paws were icy-cold on her hand.

Lindy sprawled on her bed. "Come and see what Mrs Tucker has given me," she invited. Pinky climbed up onto her stomach and settled down, still purring loudly. He stretched out his front legs and kneaded with his paws.

"Ouch. Steady with those claws," Lindy warned.

Sensitive to the tone of her voice, the young cat stopped kneading and gazed at Lindy seriously with his clear green eyes. His face wore such a wise expression, it made Lindy laugh.

"You know, Pinky," she said, gently stroking the pink nose which had prompted the tabby's name, "I think you're the loveliest little cat in the whole world – the next best thing to having my own pony."

Pinky blinked and his eyes began to close with contentment.

Lindy remembered the litter of kittens which she had discovered back in the spring. She had found them in the hay barn, tucked away in a warm corner – five tiny, mewing kittens with stumpy tails and closed eyes, huddled together in the hay. There were two black ones, two gingers and one tabby. At first, Lindy thought that they had been abandoned, and she wondered whether she could feed them all, using an old doll's bottle. However, soon a dark shape had appeared at the entrance to the barn. The mother, twitching her tail nervously, stood hesitantly in the spring sunshine.

Lindy knew that the cat would come no closer while she was there – the farm cats lived and slept outside and were half wild. She climbed up into the bales of hay and lay, as still and as quiet as she could, watching the kittens and waiting for the black mother cat to return to her family. She soon did this, and Lindy watched the kittens stumbling to nestle against and feed from their mother, who lay down in the hay beside them. Each kitten was then carefully licked clean and soon the five kittens were fast asleep, while the mother cat rested and watched.

Lindy crept away quietly and at suppertime she told her father about her find.

"That'll be Blackie," Dad said. "Reckon it'll be her first litter – she's not much more than a kitten herself! She's a good mouser, that one."

Dad did not believe in pets in the house. He liked animals, but they had to pay their way.

"There's no room for sentiment in farming," he was fond of saying.

Lindy loved old Bess, the black and white Border Collie who rounded up the cattle for Dad and Jim every morning and evening, and many times on a freezing winter's night Lindy had asked Dad if Bess could come in by the fire.

Dad, however, was adamant. "She's a

working dog, Lindy," he would say. "Makes 'em soft, bringing them into the house. Dogs *like* to work – old Bess is happy enough."

And so Bess stayed out in her straw bed in the barn, and Lindy continued to long for a pet of her own – most of all, a pony.

It was Mum who had started her on the Pony Fund. Mum had been sympathetic. "But we just can't afford it, love," she had explained. "It's such hard work, keeping a farm going." She had thought for a moment. "But, Lindy," she had said, slowly, "why don't you start saving your pocket money and any other money – Christmas and birthday? Perhaps you could save enough for your own pony, one day."

Lindy had been very excited about Mum's idea.

"They cost a lot of money, though," she had reminded her mother.

But Mum was not to be daunted. "Then, why not save for a foal and train it yourself," she had suggested. "I'll help. I'm sure Dad would agree to *that*. The pony, when you've trained it, would be worth much more than the foal."

That had seemed such a wonderful

idea that they had danced with delight around the kitchen, ending in a collapsed heap of laughter on Dad's chair by the range.

Tears sprang to Lindy's eyes when she remembered how Mum had helped her – had paid her a few pence for jobs that Lindy would have done anyway.

Dad had agreed, in principle, to the idea of saving for a foal, and the Pony Fund had grown, as had Lindy's desire for her own pony. But when Mum died Lindy lost interest in everything, and it was Pinky who helped her recover.

She had returned again and again to the hay barn and the little cat family. Although still on her guard, Blackie allowed Lindy to stroke and play with the kittens. Their eyes were now open and they were becoming more venturesome, climbing amongst the hay bales and pouncing on the insects which had also made their home in the hay.

From the start, Lindy had been drawn to the little tabby kitten. She spent more and more time, during those Easter holidays, sitting high up in the bales of hay, playing with Pinky.

Dad had found her there, one sunny April morning. He was glad that, at last,

Lindy seemed to be coming out of the cocoon of misery in which she had hidden since her mother's death. He smiled at the antics of the kittens, who were now six weeks old.

"She's a clever little cat, that Blackie," he remarked. "I should really have drowned her kittens as soon as they were born, but she hid them well. Don't worry," he added hastily, seeing the fear jump into Lindy's eyes. "They're grown now, and they're tame, thanks to you. We shall have to try and find homes for them." He smiled again, seeing Lindy gather the tabby kitten towards her, protectively.

"Lindy," he said, gently, "would you like to keep the tabby for your own – having him in the house, like you're always wanting old Bess?"

Deserting the kitten, Lindy scrambled down from the hay bales and flung her arms around her father's neck.

"Oh, thank you, Dad – of *course* I would!"

Suddenly the day seemed brighter and life had improved from then on – until the day that Dad announced his intention to marry Susan.

*

As Lindy sat in her bedroom on that cold December evening, with a whining winter wind rattling her window and moaning through the treetops, she tried to puzzle out her antagonistic feelings towards Susan.

"Oh Pinky," she sighed, "I wish I could make myself like Susan." She gazed towards the Pony Fund book, remembering how Mum had given her the first tenpence piece to start it off. "But I'm not having her trying to take Mum's place," she added, fiercely.

Pinky continued to purr his agreement, although his eyes were closed. Lindy rubbed his head. "Wake up, little puss," she urged. "I must tell you. I've got it at last – the fifty pounds." Pinky opened two green slits and then closed his eyes again.

"And Dad's going to take me to Yatebury Market next Wednesday," Lindy told him, happily. She forgot her rebellious feeling towards Susan, as she turned the pages of the Pony Fund book.

"There we are," she murmured. "Forty-nine pounds, sixty-three pence." Quickly scribbling in the new entry of sixty pence, she wrote the total of fifty pounds, twenty-three pence, and underlined it twice.

"There," she said, triumphantly, leaning back against her headboard, "I've made it, Mum – fifty pounds!"

Lindy closed her eyes and allowed herself to dream. She could hear her mother's voice saying, "Aim for fifty pounds, Lindy – I should think you could find a nice little foal for that – perhaps at the beginning of the winter when people don't want the expense of feeding."

Lindy's mind took her on to Yatebury Market next Wednesday, and there in the ring was a beautiful little chestnut foal, gazing at her from big, round eyes, stretching his neck towards her inquisitively and pushing into her hand with his soft baby muzzle . . .

CHAPTER THREE

Kate and Snuffles

The next morning, bright winter sunshine sparkled on frost-covered grass and hedges, and the air was sharp and clear. Pinky, with the frost in his toes, danced across the cobbled yard, chasing a late autumn leaf, as Lindy let herself out through the front door. She had managed to avoid Susan this morning, helping herself to Cornflakes and milk while Susan was outside at the back of the farmhouse, letting out the hens, feeding them and collecting the eggs. This had been a job which Lindy had enjoyed helping with but now, sullenly, she kept away. Susan had been at the farm for less than a week, but already Lindy was building up an invisible barrier between them.

This morning, however, Lindy had other things to think about. It was Saturday, and Kate was coming, with Snuffles. Kate lived in Hackerton, three miles away, and she and Lindy were both in the Fourth Year at Hackerton Primary School. They shared a common passion for ponies, and had spent many hours at school in past years, tying each other to skipping ropes and cantering around the playground, shaking their heads and neighing loudly.

Last summer, Kate's parents had finally succumbed and presented their delighted daughter with Snuffles, a fat, naughty and adorable grey Welsh Mountain pony. Kate, cheerful and generous-hearted, shared her pony happily with Lindy, and the two girls had spent much of last summer together.

Lindy had not seen Kate since half-term, for Kate had had a sharp attack of chicken-pox, unusually late in the year, and had been away from school for a month.

Now, Lindy could see Snuffles' ample form, ambling down the lane towards her, with Kate perched on top; she hurried to meet them.

"Hi!" Kate called, cheerfully. "We've taken *hours* to get here – Snuffles is *really* lazy today." Kate's round face was pink with exertion. Snuffles placidly ignored her attempts at squeezing him into a trot, even though these attempts were more in the form of kicks.

"Perhaps it's the cold weather," Lindy said, putting an arm round Snuffles' neck. "It *has* gone cold very suddenly." Lindy loved Snuffles, with his mischievous brown eyes and his little pointed ears which were almost hidden beneath a thatch of white mane which grew in all directions. She was forever making excuses for his lovably wicked ways.

Kate laughed at her friend's excuse.

"He's just fat and lazy," she chuckled, patting his neck. She pulled on the reins and Snuffles obligingly came to a halt. She slid down from the saddle. "Do you want to ride him?" she asked, handing over the reins. "My legs are worn out." She took off her hard hat and shook out her dark hair. "Here you are," she said, handing Lindy the hat. "Better wear this."

"Thanks," said Lindy, pushing the hat firmly onto her head. "I forgot mine – it's such a long time since I rode."

She unbuckled the stirrup leathers and lowered them by a hole, for she had longer legs than Kate. Then, gathering up the reins and putting her foot in the stirrup, she jumped lightly into the saddle.

Placidly, Snuffles stood in the middle of the lane, one small pointed ear flicked back in Lindy's direction.

"Come on then, Snuffles," she urged, squeezing him with her heels. "Show us that you're not fat and lazy – just tired from walking three miles in the cold."

Snuffles stood his ground.

"You're letting me down, Snuffy," Lindy warned, kicking the little grey pony firmly in the ribs. Snuffles sighed and moved slowly away. He snorted, sending a plume of smoky breath into the frosty air.

"It's lovely to be riding again," Lindy said.

"You ought to have come over while I was in bed," Kate said. "I felt awful for a while – I just didn't feel like riding. I've been able to ride for the last two weeks, but Miss Matthews didn't want me back at school until I was out of quarantine." Kate grinned. "Wasn't that a shame!" she added, wickedly.

"And Dad wouldn't let me come over in case I caught it," Lindy said. "It's been a bit hectic here, anyway," she added, "with Dad getting married. I went to stay with Aunt Madge in Yatebury while Dad and Susan were on honeymoon."

She looked across at Kate in mock annoyance. "You were a nuisance having chicken-pox – I could have stayed with you, instead."

Kate pulled a face. "I didn't enjoy it, *I* can tell you – except afterwards, when I was just in quarantine." She turned to look up at Lindy. "What's she like?" she asked.

"Who?"

"Susan, of course, silly. Is she nice?"

Lindy sighed and looked straight ahead. "She's all right, I suppose," she admitted, grudgingly. Then she turned flashing eyes on Kate. "But she's not going to take Mum's place, that's all I know."

Kate was silent, seeing that she had touched on a difficult subject. They reached the farm entrance and turned in through the two high, wooden gates.

"Did you manage to get a jump up?" Kate asked.

"Oh yes," Lindy replied eagerly, giving Snuffles his head down the cobbled slope into the yard, "Jim helped me. It's a bit rickety, but it'll do."

The two girls spent the rest of the morning trying to persuade a somewhat unenthusiastic Snuffles to attempt the small brush jump that Lindy and Jim had fixed up in the orchard. Snuffles had his eyes firmly fixed on the long grass, so different from the nibbled turf in his own field. When, at last, the brush fence looked in danger of being demolished completely, Lindy and Kate admitted defeat.

"Snuffles, you *are* hard work sometimes," Kate panted, sliding down from the saddle and snatching at the bridle to stop the little grey pony from reaching down at the grass. "Oh, no you don't," she warned. "Not until I've taken off your bridle. I don't want to clean that bit again, just yet!"

Lindy was already unbuckling the girth and pushing the stirrups up the leathers.

"Are you sure it's all right to leave him in the orchard?" Kate asked, as she undid the throat lash. "He's dying to get at that grass."

Snuffles rolled his brown eyes wickedly towards the grass, while Kate held on firmly to the reins.

"Of course," Lindy replied. She threw the loose girth over and lifted the saddle from Snuffles' back, propping it against a nearby apple tree.

Free at last, Snuffles put his head down

and tore at the grass with his teeth as if there were no tomorrow.

"Poor little Snuffles," Lindy said, patting his shoulder. "You don't like jumping much, do you?"

"He's *hopeless* at it!" Kate said, bluntly. "I don't know why I bother."

Always ready to spring to his defence, Lindy said, "But think how good he is at musical chairs and bending."

The two friends looked towards the shaggy little Welsh Mountain pony and remembered the fun that they had had during the summer at local gymkhanas. In the gymkhana games, Snuffles had, indeed, found a pastime which he enjoyed. The excitement of competition seemed to enter his blood as he twisted and turned round the bending poles, or galloped for a vacant chair in musical chairs. He seemed to understand exactly what was expected of him. In the potato race, he stretched out his short neck and raced for the bucket, pulling up sharply but carefully to allow the potato to be dropped into the bucket, before wheeling round to race back again. Usually he came home with several rosettes fluttering from his bridle.

"Yes, it's true he's not bad at gymkhana

games," Kate admitted, giving Snuffles an affectionate rub before turning to pick up the saddle. "But come on," she added, turning towards the farmhouse. "Tell me all about your Pony Fund – do you *really* think you'll be able to buy a foal?"

Kate decided to set off for home at half past two.

"Mum fusses if I'm not home well before dark," she sighed, as she eased the bit into Snuffles' mouth. Snuffles chewed on the cold metal, while Kate settled the headpiece in position amongst his thick, untidy mane. She pulled wisps of forelock from under the headband and buckled the throat lash.

"I bet you enjoyed that grass," Kate said fondly, tickling his grey nose. Snuffles snorted, but stood patiently. One thing that Snuffles was good about was being caught. An eternal optimist, he always thought that a meal was in the offing, and came eagerly to the call. He was also patient and obedient when he was being groomed and saddled.

"There's a good boy," Kate said. "Time for home now."

"You ride him, Lindy," she added,

turning to her friend. "He'll probably go a bit faster, now he's pointing in the direction of home!"

"Thanks," Lindy said, climbing up into the saddle. "I'll go with you as far as the main road."

Susan came to the back door of the farm as Snuffles clattered through the yard. Kate followed him, pushing Lindy's old bike, which rattled noisily across the cobbles.

"Goodbye, Kate," Susan called. "Come again won't you!"

"Bye, Mrs Cottham," Kate replied. "Yes, I will. Thanks for the lunch – it was lovely."

Susan smiled. "Any time," she called.

Lindy glanced in her direction and thought she caught a wistful look in Susan's eyes as she smiled at Kate. But why on earth should Susan look wistful?

"Be back before dark, won't you, Lindy," Susan added. "The batteries are a bit low, aren't they, on your front light?"

"OK," Lindy replied, briefly.

Out in the lane, Kate pedalled alongside Snuffles who, with his grey nose pointed towards home, was trotting gently down the lane.

"Susan seems *really* nice," Kate said, cautiously.

Lindy grunted non-committally.

Kate was silent for a while, wondering whether she should try to discuss this touchy subject or whether she should not interfere. She had known Lindy since they had both started school at the age of five, and they had been close friends for the past three years. Kate felt puzzled by Lindy's apparent dislike of her new stepmother. The silent, glowering Lindy at lunch that day had not been the friend that Kate was used to.

At last she decided to speak. "Look," she blurted out, "I know it's none of my business, but ... well ... I don't think your stepmother is trying to take your own mother's place – really I don't. I *can* understand how you must feel, but—" She stopped, wondering how Lindy would take her outburst.

Lindy turned towards her friend wearily. "Kate, I know you mean well, but after all, you *don't* know what it's like – you've still got your own mother and ..." She felt the tears rising in her eyes and rubbed them back, angrily. "I – just don't want to talk about it," she finished, flatly, turning her face away so that Kate should not see the tears that hovered in the corner of her eyes, threatening to spill down her cheeks.

Snuffles jogged on through the chill of the winter afternoon, his breath turning to smoke in the sharp air. The two girls, silent for a while, began to chat guardedly, but the mood of the day had been spoiled and Lindy was glad when they reached the main road. She slid down from the saddle.

"Thank you, Snuffles," she said, patting his thick grey neck. "It was good to be riding again." She moved the stirrup leather up a hole, while Kate did the same on the other side, checking the girth at the same time.

"Sorry about tomorrow," Kate said, as she jumped into the saddle, "but I'll be expected to give rides to the cousins all afternoon." She pulled a face as she thought of the family visit which was expected the next day. Her three young cousins were lively and demanding, and loved to be trotted up and down the drive on Snuffles. "And thanks for the jumping," she added with a grin. "If you can call it that! Hope your jump survives."

"It should do," Lindy replied. "I've

nothing to jump over it – unless perhaps I can train Pinky!"

Kate laughed. "Don't forget the foal," she said. "You'll be able to teach him, one day."

Lindy snorted. "Not for *years*," she pointed out, "and I haven't got one yet."

"You will, soon, I *know* you will," Kate replied.

Lindy stroked Snuffles' nose. "Perhaps I will," she said, dreamily. "And perhaps he'll grow up to be just like Snuffles."

"I hope not!" Kate giggled.

Snuffles cocked one ear back and snorted impatiently. It was time he was on the way home.

Kate patted his neck. "I didn't mean it, Snuffy, really I didn't." She grinned at Lindy. "I think he's offended," she said. "Perhaps I'd better take him home now and give him his tea – he might forgive me, then! See you on Monday," she called, waving goodbye, as she and Snuffles took to the main road.

CHAPTER FOUR

Misgivings

When Lindy arrived back at Court Farm, dusk was settling outside. The first star was shining above the cowsheds, where the swish of water and Jim's cheery whistling told her that milking was over and the sheds were being hosed down.

In the yard, the cows stood patiently in the twilight, waiting to be let out. Old Bess flitted in and out of the shed, excitedly, waiting for Jim to finish hosing and to open the gates, allowing her to begin her evening task of herding the cows back to their fields.

The big farmhouse kitchen was warm and lit only by the range, as Lindy entered from the hall. Pinky was sitting on the corner of the fender, blinking into the firelight. He jumped down when he saw Lindy, and trotted to meet her, miaowing a greeting. She stooped to stroke him, and he wove his way through her legs, purring and rubbing against her.

Susan came in from the scullery, carrying a tray, and then Lindy noticed that a small table and a tea-trolley had been pulled up near the fire and tea had been laid there, instead of on the big table.

Just like we used to before Mum died, Lindy thought, her heart twisting painfully.

Susan looked across at Lindy, reading her thoughts.

"I thought we could have tea by the fire. Your dad said you used to ... at weekends." She spoke awkwardly, and Lindy was surprised to find herself wanting to comfort her. There was something sad in Susan's face today – the wistfulness that Lindy had noticed earlier was still there. But, deep inside Lindy, the resentment still lurked, and she turned away to stroke Pinky.

Susan put the tray down on the table and turned to go back to the scullery.

"Can I help?" Lindy said, suddenly.

Susan looked pleased. "If you could just put those things on the table and make the tea," she said with a smile, "the kettle's on the range – I'll bring in the bread and we'll start toasting. We could even start before the others come in – just the two of us."

"OK," said Lindy, beginning to unload the tray. There were scones and strawberry jam and a sponge cake with icing. "I don't know if there'll be anything left for Jim and Dad, though, if I get first go at this lot," she added to Pinky, who blinked at her from the fender.

That night, Lindy lay awake, unable to sleep. The lecture from Kate and the expression on Susan's face had unsettled her, and thoughts kept wandering around her mind. Was she really being unfair to Susan by thinking that she wanted to take Mum's place? But she *was* supposed to be her new mother, wasn't she, and there could never be another Mum. The thoughts banged about uncomfortably in Lindy's head, and she tossed and turned. At last, she fell asleep, to dream uneasy, troubled dreams.

Sunday dawned grey and sombre, and Lindy woke to the sound of rain lashing against the window panes.

"We're lucky it's not snow, I reckon," Dad remarked, at breakfast.

"It's a bit early for snow, isn't it?" Susan commented.

"Mm. Maybe. But I think we're in for some hard weather this winter."

Lindy looked up, hopefully. *"Real* snow, do you mean, Dad, so that I can use my toboggan?" Lindy had been given a toboggan by an aunt for Christmas three years ago, but had not yet been able to use it.

Dad smiled at her across the table. "I reckon so," he said.

Lindy gazed out of the kitchen window towards Home Field, which sloped steeply towards the river. She imagined flying down the hill on her toboggan, and wondered who would come with her. Perhaps Helen from Dreybridge, the village just down the lane? But Helen was always busy; her father kept her working in all her spare time at his fruit shop, and on Sundays she did a paper round in the morning and had to help her mother in the afternoon. Poor Helen had very little time for herself.

Lindy turned her gaze away from the window, where the rain fell in a solid grey sheet. She looked at Susan.

"Do you think Kate could come to stay

in the holidays – after Christmas?" she asked.

Susan looked at Dad across the table.

"Well, don't look at me, love," Dad said. "If you can manage, I don't mind."

"Oh, she won't be any trouble," Lindy assured him. "She can sleep in my room on the camp bed, and she can bring Snuffles. Then, if it doesn't snow we can ride Snuffles, and if it does, we can toboggan!"

Dad chuckled. "You've got it all worked out, haven't you?" he laughed.

"Well, I think that sounds a lovely idea," Susan assured her, warmly. "Where is Kate today? Aren't you going to see her?"

Lindy explained about the cousins.

"Well, let's hope the weather improves anyway," Susan commented and then, turning to Lindy, she added, "So what will you do today?"

Lindy shrugged her shoulders. "Nothing much, I suppose," she said. "I've got some homework to do."

Susan hesitated. Then she said, "I'm going to make the Christmas puddings this afternoon. Would you like to help me?"

It was Lindy's turn to hesitate. "Oh, I

don't know," she said, at last. "I'll see how my homework goes." Gathering Pinky up in her arms, she escaped back to her bedroom, to brood over the Pony Account book and to gaze out through her rain-splattered window.

CHAPTER FIVE

You're Not Going to Yatebury!

Sitting up in her bedroom on Tuesday night, Lindy wondered, miserably, how it had all happened. She hadn't meant it to be like this.

Sunday had been quite a good day, even though the rain had continued to pour down relentlessly. Lindy had finished her term's project for Art, which was a painting of Pinky, sitting by the range. Only too pleased to be away from the bad weather, Pinky sat obligingly on the brass fender, blinking dreamily, the glowing light from the grate shining on the ginger patches in his tabby fur.

Susan, meanwhile, mixed the Christmas puddings and put them on the stove to cook, before bringing out the farm record books.

"I'm hoping to gradually get these milk records up to date," she told Lindy. "Your

Dad doesn't seem very good at record-keeping."

Lindy turned away from her painting for a moment. "He's not," she admitted. "He's good at practical things – you know, mending machinery and broken gates, that sort of thing. But—" Lindy laughed. "You should hear him when he has to do his VAT return!"

"I can imagine!" Susan chuckled. "I'll do it next time."

It had been a warm, comfortable afternoon, and Lindy felt happier than she had for months. Susan, too, had looked happy as she cleared away the record books.

How had it happened, then, Lindy asked herself again, when things had seemed to be getting better? Monday had been another good day, and today had been all right – until this evening.

When Lindy thought about it, she *had* felt rather tired and irritable this evening. Miss Matthews had been in one of her "I can't cope" moods, and had succeeded in reducing the entire 4th year to a state of near-rebellion.

Susan had seemed preoccupied that evening, and Dad and Jim had come in from milking arguing. So, really, Lindy

thought with a sigh, it was hardly sur-
prising that things had gone wrong. She
gazed glumly at her Pony Fund book, as
Dad's words echoed through her mind.

"You needn't think you're going to
Yatebury Market with me tomorrow,
young lady," he had shouted at her, his
eyes blazing, "because you're not. And
you can go to bed, *now* – this minute!"

Lindy's anger had matched his own,
and her eyes, too, were fiery as she glared
back at him. "All right," she had said,
tossing back her hair, defiantly, "I'm
going – I wouldn't want to stay here,
anyway." And she had marched across to
the door leading to the hall. As she
reached the door she became aware of
Susan standing by the range and her
anger melted a little.

It hadn't been Susan's fault; it had been
Lindy, herself, who had turned on her
when she had asked to see the Pony Fund
book. The book had been something
special between her and Mum; Susan had
seemed to be threatening that specialness,
and Lindy had turned on her, angrily.

Suddenly, Lindy realised how unfair
she had been to Susan. She turned back
and opened her mouth to speak, but Dad
spoke first.

"I told you to go to bed," he roared. "Do as you're told, at once!"

"So that's that, I suppose," Lindy said, flatly, ruffling the fur under Pinky's chin. She was sitting across the cushioned window-seat in her bedroom, her feet resting against the recess wall on one side and her back against the other. Pinky, curled comfortably on her stomach, purred back. He had had a busy afternoon hunting mice in the hay-barn, and was content to doze and listen to Lindy, occasionally opening his green eyes to gaze at her lovingly.

"Dad won't take me to Yatebury Market," Lindy continued, miserably, "so there's no hope of a foal yet – I shall have to wait . . ."

She gazed out through the half-open curtains, watching the stars glinting in the frost-clear sky. She remembered how Mum, whenever she had seen the first star, shining bright and alone in the evening sky, had always called to Lindy, "Look – the first star. Quick, Lindy, wish on it, before you see the other stars!"

And they had both closed their eyes and wished, silently, and laughed after-

41

wards because they knew that it was just a superstition. *Always*, Lindy had wished for a pony, and somewhere inside her – and perhaps in Mum, too – there had been a belief that, perhaps, the wish *might* come true . . .

"Pinky!" Lindy said, suddenly, picking him up in her arms and swinging her legs down onto the floor. "I *will* go – I *will*!"

Lindy's eyes were shining as brightly as the stars as she put a surprised Pinky down on her bed and went to the chest of drawers to fetch the cash box.

Already a plan was beginning to form in her mind . . .

Shivering as she dressed quickly in her school clothes, Lindy looked out through the window to where the dim light of dawn was paling the sky above the cow-shed roof. A delicate pattern of frost edged each window pane, and a line of white frost was just visible on the roof edge.

Pinky jumped down from Lindy's bed, where he had slept all night. He stretched, arching his back, and then sat down abruptly and began to lick the fur on his shoulders. His head moved rhythmically in quick, short jerks.

Lindy turned back to concentrate on her own preparations for the day. Fetching her school bag from the hook on her door, she pulled out the school books. Then, pulling open the bottom drawer of her chest of drawers, she took out the cash box. Taking out the money, which she had packed into a plastic bag, she pushed it into her school bag. Then, from the drawer, she took a brand-new rope halter – a birthday present, last year, from Jim. She fingered the pale rope thoughtfully, before pushing the halter down on top of the money. Next followed a pair of trousers from the second drawer, together with a sweater. She pushed the sweater well down into the bag and fastened the buckles.

"That's about it, I think, Pinky," she said, picking up the school books and packing them into the bottom drawer.

Pinky, having finished his morning wash, was standing on the window-seat, his two front paws resting on the sill. He turned to look back into the room towards Lindy, and miaowed.

"Are you *sure* you want to go out there?" Lindy asked him, walking over to the window. "It looks cold." Pinky miaowed again, rubbing his head against her hand, as she opened the window. Lindy shivered, partly from the frosty air, but partly from excitement, as she thought of the day ahead.

Pinky slipped out silently, padding softly down the sloping roof and disappearing into the greyness.

Lindy folded her pyjamas carefully and put them under her pillow. She straightened the covers on her bed, turning back the top sheet and tucking in the side. Finally, she pulled up the bedspread and smoothed it carefully, excitement bubbling inside her all the while.

Reaching up to the hook for her duffle coat and scarf, and swinging the school bag over her shoulder, she opened her bedroom door.

Dad was still out in the cowsheds when Lindy came downstairs. She could hear him clattering about in the dairy. Susan was nowhere to be seen; Jim and Old Bess were probably just at the last field, and soon they would be in for breakfast. Lindy did not want to see any of them this morning, so she quickly gulped down her Cornflakes and milk.

Susan had already laid the table for

breakfast. Lindy cut herself three slices of bread from the loaf and spread them with butter and marmalade. Pushing two slices together into a thick sandwich, she cut the sandwich and wrapped the two halves in greaseproof paper from the dresser drawer, stuffing these provisions, together with an apple from the dresser, into her school bag.

Then, pulling on her duffle coat and picking up the other piece of bread and marmalade to eat on her way, she crept out of the farmhouse through the front door. Susan was still nowhere to be seen, but Lindy knew that she might watch from the kitchen window to see the school bus stop in the lane at the bottom of Home Field. So, with her bag over her shoulder, she walked down the lane, as usual, to meet the bus.

It was cold waiting for the bus. Lindy stamped her feet and blew into her gloves. She looked over the high hedge, across Home Field to where the lights of Court Farm winked in the greyness. She could see the kitchen light, shining into the winter morning. Susan would not be able to see whether Lindy actually boarded the bus, but she might watch to see the bus pull up to collect her. Lindy was the only person to be picked up at that particular point.

At last, Lindy heard the bus winding its way creakily around the country lanes, and then it appeared round the corner and rattled to a stop beside her. Helen was sitting in the front seat, nearest to the door. Standing on the bottom step, Lindy called in to her. "I'm not going to school today – Dad arranged it with Miss Matthews."

Helen stood up and peered at Lindy, short-sightedly. She was small for her age, thin and wiry, with big, sad blue eyes that looked out from behind round, steel-rimmed glasses.

"Lucky thing!" she said. "You're going to Yatebury, aren't you, to get a foal?" Lindy nodded. "You *are* lucky," she said again.

"Skiving are we, today?" the bus driver laughed, as he heaved the old bus into first gear, ready to pull away up the slope of Dreybridge Hill. "Have a good day!" Winking at Lindy, cheerfully, he eased his foot off the clutch and the bus pulled away, noisily.

Lindy felt suddenly alone and just a little frightened, as she watched the lights

of the bus moving up the hill and disappearing over the brow.

She had never played truant before –
what would Dad say, when he found out?
Lindy comforted herself with the thought
that at least Miss Matthews was not
expecting her, and so would not wonder
where she was.

Turning back, Lindy walked slowly up
the lane. At the entrance to Court Farm,
she slipped stealthily past in the
shadows, her heart thumping uncomfortably. The one cattle truck that the farm
boasted was parked next to the hay barn
which had its own piece of land, on the
opposite side of the lane.

Throwing her school bag up into the
truck, Lindy climbed up into the back. As
she sat on the tarpaulins, the excitement
returned. She had begun it now – there
was no turning back.

Pulling out the trousers and sweater
from the bag, Lindy changed quickly out
of her school clothes and then settled herself down for a long wait, knowing that
Dad would not be out until nearly ten
o'clock. As soon as she heard him
coming, she would crawl under the
tarpaulins . . .

CHAPTER SIX

The Sale

Lindy clung to the ridges on the floor of the truck, as it lurched through the lanes. She felt sorry for the cattle when they had to travel in the truck, but maybe Dad drove more slowly then. She ventured a peep from under the tarpaulins. Squinting between the side slats of the truck, Lindy recognised Hackerton High Street. She frowned slightly – what was Dad doing in Hackerton? Surely, he was off-course for Yatebury?

The truck slowed and then came to a halt, and Lindy's heart turned over. Dad had stopped the truck outside her school! She heard his steps on the pavement.

Pulling the tarpaulins over her head again, she lay on the straw in the corner of the truck, questions racing through her mind. Why had Dad stopped here? Was he going to see Miss Matthews? Would he find out that Lindy was not at school?

Huddled miserably in her dark corner, Lindy waited.

At last, she heard Dad's returning footsteps. She held her breath. She heard him come round to the back of the truck, where he stopped and began to undo the bolt. However, he seemed to be just checking it, for then he continued on round to the cab and climbed up into the driver's seat.

Lindy felt the floor vibrating as Dad started up the engine, and then they were off again, down Hackerton High Street. Lindy poked her head out carefully from beneath the tarpaulins and watched as they passed shops, the Post Office and then Hackerton Church. The truck slowed for a corner and Lindy saw a sign pointing to the right, which read "Yatebury, 5 miles". The truck stopped at the junction and then turned slowly to the right. Dad began to whistle, and Lindy watched excitedly as hedges and fields sped by. The truck passed through two small hamlets and then, with her heart quickening, Lindy saw the sign "Yatebury". The truck slowed down to a snail's pace, as it joined a queue of traffic making for the Market. Through her peep-hole, Lindy watched as they turned into the market area and a car park attendant signalled towards the lorry park. Then, she hid again under her tarpaulins and waited while the truck came to a halt and she heard the engine stop. The cab door banged, and Lindy could hear Dad paying the attendant. She heard the crunch of his shoes on the gravel as he left the truck.

Waiting for a few minutes, Lindy emerged cautiously from beneath the tarpaulins. A careful scrutiny of the lorry park, through the side slats of the truck, showed no sign of Dad, so she stood up, thankfully, and brushed the straw from her clothes. Her legs were stiff and she was cold. Picking up her school bag, Lindy climbed out of the back of the truck and jumped down onto the gravel of the lorry park.

She was here at last! Lindy breathed in the Market-day smells of animals, vegetables and open air. The Market stalls were crowded together, and customers jostled for position in the narrow walk-ways between. Lindy set off in the direction of the livestock, keeping a sharp look out for Dad.

Threading her way slowly through the stalls and pens, Lindy's eyes searched the Market for signs of ponies or foals.

At last, she glimpsed a pony's head, through the crowds. She pushed her way through, determinedly, past groups of farmers laughing and joking; past farmers' wives, warmly dressed and gossiping gently; past pens – one filled with hissing geese, another with fat, grunting pigs. Warmer by now, Lindy reached the ring, where a pony was being paraded, whilst others stood nearby. Lindy's eyes searched the rows and her spirits dropped as no foals came into view.

A young black pony, about thirteen hands, pranced round the ring, led by a brown-haired man. Lindy watched admiringly as the pony tossed his head and shied sideways at something in the crowd which frightened him.

What a lovely pony that would be to own and ride – young and full of life. Lindy allowed herself a momentary daydream, as she galloped the black pony across Home Field, hearing his hooves thudding on the grass, seeing his black mane tossed by the wind.

"Going . . . Going . . . Gone! Sold to the gentleman for two hundred pounds!"

The Auctioneer's voice, flat and emotionless, brought Lindy's thoughts back to real life. As the black pony pranced out of the ring, Lindy sighed. She must be practical. Two hundred pounds for a pony was quite out of her reach. She pushed her way through the crowd to the Auctioneer's rostrum. He was busy writing his notes.

"Excuse me." Lindy's voice came almost as a whisper, and the Auctioneer continued to scribble. Annoyed at herself for being so nervous, Lindy cleared her throat and tried again.

"Excuse me!" This time, it was a shout, and the Auctioneer jumped, turning to look down towards Lindy over the top of his glasses.

"I'm not deaf, you know," he said, irritably. Peering down at Lindy, he added, more kindly, "What can I do for you, Miss?"

"Well . . ."

"Come on, now. I haven't got all day." The Auctioneer looked harassed as he glanced towards the row of waiting ponies.

"Have you any foals to be auctioned?" Lindy blurted out.

The Auctioneer pushed the glasses back up onto his nose and peered at his notes. "Foals . . . let's have a look . . . can't see any."

Lindy's hopes, already dwindling, disappeared completely. Seeing her dejected expression, the Auctioneer added, "But just to make sure, go and see that man over there." He turned round and pointed behind him. "The one with the white coat."

Thanking him, Lindy crossed over to where the man in the white coat stood. He had a round, cheerful face, with brown eyes that smiled at Lindy when she asked him her question.

"Are you selling any foals today, please?"

"Well now, my dear, I'm afraid not," he replied, "I'm sorry to disappoint you. What age foal did you want?"

Lindy told him about her fifty pounds, and about Mum's suggestion of buying a young foal at this time of year, when the owners did not want to pay for their keep.

The man nodded, understandingly. "Yes . . . well, we did have a couple last year, I remember," he said, "but not this year, I'm afraid." He leaned forward. "You want to come back to our June Market – you'd mebbe find a nice yearling then." He rubbed his chin, reflectively. "Give you time to save up a bit more, too.

"I do know someone who's selling his young colt," he added, "but he's looking for nearer a hundred pounds for it."

Dejectedly, Lindy wandered away, her heart heavy. It was no good, then. She had played truant from school for nothing – and she still had Dad to face. Not really caring where she went, Lindy found herself wandering towards the line of ponies. Her eyes travelled over them – a dapple grey cob, a bay pony with wild eyes, a thin, nervous-looking chestnut. Then her eyes settled on a nondescript brown pony, standing as still as a statue. Lindy's attention was arrested by the sight of this pony. Something about the way it stood, one hind leg resting and its head drooping miserably, caught at her heart. She wandered over, studying the pony as she walked. It looked as if no one had ever bothered to groom it – its brown coat was caked with mud and its mane and tail were tangled and knotted.

"Hello, little pony," Lindy ventured, gently, as she arrived beside the brown pony. The pony did not move, but one ear flicked back in Lindy's direction.

Lindy lifted a tentative hand to stroke

the mud-caked neck, and the pony turned its head slowly towards her. Large, kind eyes looked at her, dejectedly, from under a long, black forelock, and Lindy's heart was lost.

"What a lovely old girl you are," she told the pony, patting her and rubbing her behind the ears. She patted the pony's shoulders and felt the thinness beneath the little mare's thick winter coat. Her eyes noted, with dismay, the pony's sunken flanks and its thin neck.

"You poor little thing – you must be hungry." Lindy remembered her sandwiches, and pulled them out from her school bag. She watched as the brown pony snatched eagerly at this unexpected meal.

"I don't think I've ever fed a pony with marmalade sandwiches before," Lindy told the pony when the last crumb had disappeared into the pony's mouth. The brown pony pushed her nose into Lindy's hand, hopefully. Lindy pulled out the apple from her bag and gave that to the pony, too. The pony crunched it hungrily.

"Sorry – it's all gone now." Lindy put her arm round the pony's neck, and her heart ached with longing.

"Excuse me, Miss." The brown-haired man appeared at Lindy's elbow. He undid the halter rope. "Time for this one to go in the ring."

Lindy's heart lurched, painfully, as the brown pony was led away. She followed, thoughts tumbling over themselves in her mind. It *was* a small and thin-looking pony, but surely fifty pounds *couldn't* be enough? She had to try, though. Lindy pushed her way through to the ringside. There was the brown pony, being led around the ring. Its head hung and it walked with a tired, dragging step. The brown-haired man tugged at the halter rope impatiently, and the pony forced itself into a slow jog, before subsiding again to its plodding walk.

"Not much life in *that*!" a farmer called out, and a slight titter ran round the watching crowd.

The Auctioneer banged his hammer. "What am I offered, then, Ladies and Gentlemen, for this ... er ... *quiet* little mare?" His eyes darted around the ring. "Come on, now. What am I offered for this one – a perfect first pony. A hundred, shall we start with?"

Lindy felt her face go pale. A hundred pounds! There was no hope, then.

Across the ring, a farmer in an old rain-coat and a battered tweed hat raised his hand, nonchalantly.

"Forty quid," he said, and Lindy's hope returned.

"Forty pounds I'm bid," came the Auctioneer's bored voice. "Let's get going, Ladies and Gentlemen." He looked at his watch. "Time's getting on. Now, you know this pony must be worth more. What am I bid? Fifty?"

Shaking, Lindy raised her hand, and the Auctioneer looked at her over his glasses for the second time that day.

"Is that a bid, young lady?"

Lindy nodded, unable to speak.

The Auctioneer turned his attention to the farmer, and Lindy's heart stood still.

"Fifty pounds I'm bid – will you make it sixty?"

The farmer looked the brown pony over. "Fifty-five, then," he said, languidly.

Lindy felt tears rush to her eyes. Through her misery, she heard the Auctioneer's voice calling, "Fifty-five I'm bid, can I have sixty pounds?" He looked towards Lindy, who shook her head, turning away to hide her tears. As she pushed her way back, away from the ring, she heard the Auctioneer's voice.

"Sixty pounds it is, then – can I have sixty-five?"

Lindy stumbled through the crowds, half blinded by her unshed tears. The talk and laughter around her now sounded harsh and cruel. She felt so miserable and alone. She decided to go straight back to the truck and wait until Dad arrived, and she began to walk towards the park. She could hide again under the tarpaulins and maybe Dad would never know that she had played truant from school and had come to Yatebury Market, after all.

Her shoulders drooping dejectedly, she plodded back down the pathway between the stalls; past the pigs and the hissing geese. Then Lindy hesitated, as she thought of the thin brown pony. Perhaps she could just go back to give it a last pat – she could even buy it something to eat with her money, since she could not buy the pony itself. Abruptly, Lindy turned round and bumped into someone. Looking up to apologise, she found herself gazing straight into Dad's face!

CHAPTER SEVEN

A Surprise

Dad had not seemed angry – not even the slightest bit cross. His eyes had twinkled as he had looked down at her.

"You're a long way from Hackerton, aren't you?" was all he said.

Lindy was almost speechless with puzzlement as she stammered a reply. Dad threw back his head and laughed heartily, and Lindy was even more puzzled.

Still chuckling, Dad explained. "I went to school this morning to fetch you," he said. "Susan persuaded me that I was being too hard on you, so I called in at Hackerton to pick you up and bring you to Yatebury Market."

"But ... surely Miss Matthews ... " Lindy began.

"Yes. Miss Matthews said that you weren't at school today, and that you had gone to Yatebury Market. Then I came out to the truck and I saw the end of your scarf sticking out from underneath the tarpaulins."

Dad began to chuckle again. "You little monkey," he laughed, catching hold of her hand and leading her towards the refreshment stand. "I couldn't be cross. I remembered that I did almost the same thing when I was a boy. I'll tell you about it some day," he added. "But just now, I'm going to buy us both a hot dog."

As Lindy watched the sausages sizzling in the hot fat, she suddenly felt very hungry. Dad had onions with his sausage and Lindy poured tomato ketchup over hers.

Then she remembered the brown pony. "Please," she asked the stall attendant, "can I buy just a roll, without the sausage?"

"What do you want that for?" Dad asked, as the man handed out a roll from behind the counter.

"It's for a poor little pony," Lindy explained. "It's *so* thin, Dad."

"I'll buy the roll for you, then," said Dad. "We can't have thin ponies around the place."

As Lindy bit into her hot dog, she looked up at Dad with puzzled brown eyes. Dad had a strange look about him that she could not quite understand.

"Have you bought anything?" she asked.

Dad looked pleased with himself. "Yes, I've bought Susan those twenty-five new pullets that she wanted," he replied. "Quite a good price, too."

Lindy kept thinking about the brown pony. "Can I go and find the pony now, Dad?" she asked, licking the last of the tomato ketchup from her fingers. "I just want to give it this roll and say goodbye."

"All right then, love – meet me back here in ten minutes, will you? I've got to arrange for those pullets to be packed in the truck."

The pony had been tied up in the same place. She turned her head wearily when Lindy spoke, and when Lindy broke the roll and fed it to her, she ate hungrily.

"Oh, I *do* hope someone is going to love you, little pony," Lindy murmured, putting her arm around its neck. The pony pushed its soft muzzle into her hand.

"Goodness me, it's *you* again!"

Lindy looked up to see the brown-haired man looking down at her and grinning.

"Every time I come to take this one away," he laughed, "you're feeding it."

"Oh – does she have to go now?" Lindy's heart began to ache again.

"I'm afraid so." The brown-haired man undid the halter rope. "I've got to load it up for the new owner."

Lindy stroked the pony's neck again and watched sadly as it was led away. Then she wandered slowly back to the refreshment stand to wait for Dad.

What a strange day it had been, Lindy thought, as she leaned against the stand. This morning, she had been so full of hope as she had put the fifty pounds into her school bag. Now, she was returning home with the fifty pounds still intact, and with a heavy heart. She wished that she had not ever *seen* the thin brown pony, for she knew that she would keep thinking about her, wondering if she was being looked after.

When Dad arrived, Lindy looked up at him. "Are we going now?" she asked.

Dad slipped his arm through hers. "Yes," he said, "we'll go home soon. I think I've bought all I'm going to for today – but I just want you to come over to the flower stall with me and help me to choose a plant for Susan."

Together, they chose a lovely pink Poinsettia, which the stall-holder said was sometimes called a Christmas Star.

"What a lovely name!" Lindy said, looking at the long, pink petals. She felt a small surge of excitement as she remembered that Christmas was only two weeks away. Seeing a pot of growing bulbs, with leaves just poking up above the soil, she decided to buy it for Mrs Tucker.

"Perhaps we should look around – we could do some Christmas shopping," Dad suggested. "You haven't looked at all the stalls yet, have you?"

Lindy, with her first Christmas present tucked under her arm, felt the glow of Christmas excitement. "That's a good idea – I'll borrow from my Pony Fund and do all my Christmas shopping!"

An hour later, their arms full of parcels, Lindy and Dad made their way back to the lorry park. Lindy could hardly see round her packages. Dad stopped as they reached the truck, and dug into his pockets for the keys.

"Well, Lindy love, I'm glad you came

after all," he said, looking down at her with twinkling eyes. "You can travel home in the front seat by me, this time, can't you?"

Lindy grinned. "Are you sure you don't want me to go back under the tarpaulins?" she said, wickedly.

"I don't think there's very much room for you, back there, now," Dad replied.

"Oh – the pullets, you mean. Surely they don't take up all the room?"

"Well . . . I bought one or two other things," Dad admitted. "I bought a Christmas tree . . ."

Lindy's eyes lit up. "Is it a big one? Has it got roots?" she asked.

"Go and have a look," Dad said, opening the cab door and beginning to unload his presents.

Still with her parcels piled up in her arms, Lindy walked round to the back of the truck and peered in. Her eyes took in the spiky green branches of the tree behind the crate of clucking pullets on the left hand side of the truck. But on the right hand side, where only a few hours earlier Lindy had huddled beneath the tarpaulins, the partitions had been erected, forming a straw-covered compartment. In the dim depths of the truck, an animal moved in the straw.

Lindy nearly dropped her parcels.

"Dad!" she squeaked, her eyes round with disbelief. It *couldn't* be – it just *couldn't* be!

Dad appeared at her side. "What's the matter?" he asked, with forced innocence. "Don't you like the Christmas tree?"

Lindy, her arms full, could only jerk her head towards the back of the truck.

"Dad – what is it?" Her voice was little more than a whisper. "It can't be, of course, but it looks like . . ."

"The thin brown pony!" Dad finished the sentence for her, triumphantly. "Yes, it is – she's yours now, Lindy!"

CHAPTER EIGHT

Gypsy

"So you've been watching me all day!" Lindy had to shout to make herself heard over the roar of the old truck's noisy engine, as Dad changed gear to negotiate the winding country lanes out of Yatebury.

Dad took his eyes off the road for a moment to grin at his daughter. "Not exactly," he laughed. "I just thought I would have a look for you. It was lucky I saw you when I did – otherwise old Sid Keevers might have bought your pony."

"The man with the tweed hat?"

"That's the one. Bit of a shifty character is Sid Keevers. I don't like to see animals going in his direction."

"Why not, Dad?" Lindy asked.

Dad looked towards her again, quickly, and this time his face was serious. "He doesn't much care how he looks after his animals," he explained. "And I've no doubt that your pony would have been on the way to the knacker's yard pretty soon. I thought I'd just give it a try, since you seemed to want the pony so much. I just tried an extra five pounds on top of Sid Keevers' bid and I got it!" Dad was silent for a while. "Come to think of it," he said pensively, "judging from the condition of the pony, it might have come from Sid Keevers' farm and he was trying to put the price up higher than he would have had for the pony as horse meat."

Lindy shuddered. "Poor little pony," she breathed. She turned her head and looked for the hundredth time through the small opening to the back of the truck. Two brown ears and a mass of untidy mane were all that she could see, but it was enough to reassure her.

Lindy turned round and looked towards Dad again. "I shan't be able to pay you back just yet," she warned him.

Dad gave her a quick glance and then kept his eyes on the road as he said, "You don't have to, love. That's your Christmas present from me."

There had been no difficulty in choosing a name for the little brown pony. Lindy had led her round to see Mrs Tucker, and the old lady's eyes had lit up when she saw her.

"Just like our little Gypsy," she had said, her eyes misting over.

Lindy was delighted. "Of course!" she said. "That's what I'll call her – Gypsy!"

That night, Lindy lay awake, unable to sleep. The day's events crowded through her mind, and always her thoughts returned to the astonishing realisation that, outside in the orchard, stood Gypsy, her very own pony!

At last, in the early hours of Thursday morning, Lindy fell asleep, only to wake with a start at six o'clock. For a moment, she wondered why she had woken so early, and then she remembered. Dressing quickly, she let herself out of her bedroom and hurried downstairs.

Susan was in the kitchen. "Hullo," she said, smiling. "I was wondering if you might be up early this morning. I had a peep over the wall just now – she's still there!"

After the argument on Tuesday evening, and the excitement of yesterday, Lindy felt strangely shy towards Susan. The barrier of resentment had somehow been replaced by another barrier of tension, which Lindy could not quite understand. "I still can't believe it's all real," she told Susan. "I must go out and see Gypsy, just to make sure."

"Take her some more hay," Susan called to Lindy, who was already pulling on her wellington boots in the scullery. "She's eaten all that we gave her last night – she must be ravenous!"

As Lindy opened the scullery door, the blast of cold air was real enough. A wintry dawn was just beginning to break in the eastern sky, making enough light for Lindy to see her way across the yard to the outhouse where Dad had left her a bale of hay. In the far corner of the yard, next to the cowsheds, the herd of Friesians was just visible; a dark mass of patient cows, with their heads turned towards the light in the shed. As Lindy hurried across to the outhouse, some cows came plodding out of the cowsheds, and she heard Dad calling the next ones in.

"Hey oop. Come on Buttercup, bring 'em in. Come on, Sorrell." There was a movement amongst the waiting cows, as Buttercup led the next batch into the sheds to be milked.

Lindy loved the cows. They were

patient, gentle creatures, and she liked helping Jim to bring them in from the fields. It was a soothing, unhurried pastime, wandering behind those gently plodding cloven hooves and the long tails which swished to and fro like pendulums.

But this morning, Lindy had other matters on her mind. With her arms full of hay, she hurried through the yard and climbed the gate into the orchard. It was still very dark, but Lindy's eyes were adjusting, and she could see the gnarled shapes of the old apple trees. She peered into the gloom, saw a dark shape and heard the tearing of grass.

As Lindy came near, Gypsy raised her head and gave a gentle whicker of recognition.

"Hello, little pony." Lindy's heart filled with pride. Never mind if this little brown pony was thin and shabby, she was her very own. "Here's some more hay for you." Lindy led the way to the three-sided shed which stood in the corner of the orchard, with Gypsy following behind.

"I'll buy you a hay net as soon as I can," she promised as she heaped the hay in the corner of the shed, "But first of all I'm going to buy you some pony nuts."

With her arm leaning on Gypsy's painfully thin withers, Lindy talked to her, watching as the pony pulled at the hay. She could have stayed there all day, feeling the warmth of Gypsy's thin body and with the pony's steady munching filling the air, as the dawn light slowly spread in the east.

Susan's voice calling her brought Lindy back to reality. Leaving Gypsy munching at the hay, she made her way back across the orchard to the farmhouse kitchen.

"I thought I'd better call you," said Susan, "or you might stay there for ever! How was she?"

"She knew me – she whickered!" Lindy looked at Susan. "I wish Dad would let me put her in the stable – just for a while until she's looking better."

"I know," Susan agreed, "but it's so expensive once you start keeping them in. She'll improve with good feeding."

"Mm. I suppose so." With one eye on the clock, Lindy hurried through her breakfast. She had stayed with Gypsy for longer than she had realised, and school bus time was approaching rapidly.

As Lindy rushed upstairs for her school

bag, she heard the click of the letterbox and when she ran down the stairs, two at a time, Susan was walking slowly back from the front door, leafing through the post.

"More Christmas cards?" Lindy called, as she reached the bottom of the stairs.

Susan looked up and Lindy was surprised to see again the wistful expression that she had seen on Susan's face on the day of Kate's visit.

"Yes," Susan replied, flatly. "More Christmas cards."

As Lindy ran down the lane in the still-dark, frosty morning, she puzzled over Susan's sad expression. She wondered if she, herself, could be the cause, and she resolved to try to be more helpful. The bus turned the corner just as Lindy reached the gate, and soon she was inside, telling Helen all about yesterday's events.

CHAPTER NINE

The Blizzard

The next two weeks flew by. The school play, the end of term and looking after Gypsy took all Lindy's time. Each night, she dropped into bed, exhausted, with just a sleepy "goodnight" to Pinky.

Lindy tried to be more friendly to Susan, and certainly the antagonism between them had disappeared. She noticed, though, how Susan looked hopefully through the post every morning, and then came the bleak expression of disappointment. Lindy longed to ask her what it was that she was waiting for, but somehow she could not bring herself to break the feeling of reserve between them.

On Christmas Eve morning, Dad brought the Christmas tree into the kitchen from the shed where it had been kept, standing in water, since Yatebury Market day.

"No good bringing it into the house too early," Dad had said, "or it'll be dropping needles everywhere before Christmas."

Susan followed behind, staggering under the weight of a large, wooden tub. She dropped it with a bang in the corner of the kitchen. "Goodness," she exclaimed, "it was heavier than I thought!" Regaining her breath, she added, "I've lined it with polythene so that we can put the tree in earth."

"Then we can plant it outside after Christmas," Lindy said, eagerly.

"Mm. I hope so. We'll have to keep it watered."

"Lovely," Lindy commented, carrying the Christmas decoration box over to the corner. "I hate to see Christmas trees thrown out after Christmas – it seems cruel!"

Dad laughed as he pulled his boots on again. "You'll be giving it a name next," he chuckled.

"Christopher!" Susan replied, promptly, laughing too.

Lindy and Susan sat companionably on the floor in the corner of the kitchen, decorating the tree, and the rest of the day passed happily and quickly.

At dusk, when Lindy went out to see

Gypsy for the last time that day, she gave her an extra large feed of pony nuts, as well as an armful of hay. Gypsy was still thin, but was beginning to fill out a little. Lindy thought longingly of the day when she would ride her. Kate had promised the loan of Snuffy's saddle and bridle, when she came to stay after Christmas, and so Lindy contented herself with grooming Gypsy's dark brown coat. Her matted coat and tangled mane and tail had taken many hours of work, but now her coat was smooth and every strand of her tail was tangle-free. Lindy had trimmed the end of the tail with the kitchen scissors.

"I'm going to save up for a bridle for you," Lindy promised the little pony, who was pushing her nose into the bucket, searching for the last pony nuts. "And then a saddle." Lindy leaned against the wall of the shed and gazed at her pony, fondly. She still could not quite believe that Gypsy was really hers.

"Then, when the summer comes," Lindy continued, dreamily, "we'll go to gymkhanas with Kate and Snuffles . . ."

As Lindy day-dreamed, Gypsy pushed at the empty bucket impatiently with her nose. She moved uneasily around the shed and pawed at the bucket.

"You can't have any more pony nuts just now," Lindy told her. "You'll have to be content with hay." She offered the pony a handful. "It's Dad's *best* hay, you know," she added. But Gypsy snorted impatiently and moved to the open side of the shed, gazing into the darkness.

Dad's voice floated across the yard, calling her in for supper so, with a last hug for Gypsy, Lindy turned towards the farmhouse. Gypsy, with a sigh, walked back into the shed and began pulling idly at the hay.

Leaving her boots just inside the scullery, Lindy pushed open the door. The big, comfortable old kitchen glowed with light from the range and from the Christmas tree, where Jim had hung the tree lights. Lindy felt the glow within her, too. Then she remembered, with sudden sadness, the Christmas just after Mum had died. What a terrible time it had been. There had been no Christmas tree, no Christmas carols wafting from the radio; just the three of them, trying desperately to be cheerful, and a trip to Aunt Madge's house for a Christmas dinner which none of them had wanted.

"Come on Lindy," said a voice, gently, and Lindy looked up to see Susan looking at her with understanding in her eyes. Thankfully, Lindy's thoughts returned to the present, and she smiled at Susan. She had a sudden urge to tell Susan how much happier Christmas was this year; to tell her how glad she was that the old farmhouse heard laughter again. She wanted to tell Susan that she was not filled with resentment any more; that she understood, now, that Susan had not wanted to take Mum's place, for Mum's place would always be there, in Lindy's heart.

All this travelled through Lindy's mind as she stood, uncertainly, in the doorway. But then the shyness returned, and instead she wandered over towards the kitchen table, where red-berried holly decorated the supper table, and where Dad was opening a bottle of his home-made elderberry wine.

In the evening, they sang Christmas carols, and it was half past eleven when Dad said, at last, "Come on, young Lindy – time for bed. I've still got to be up at five o'clock to milk the cows, you know."

Half asleep already, and with Pinky in her arms, Lindy made her way to bed. It was cold in her bedroom, and she shivered as she padded over to close the curtains. Then she saw the snow, falling gently, thinly covering the roof outside her window. She nearly ran back downstairs to tell everyone, but instead she climbed into bed and fell fast asleep.

When Lindy opened her eyes again, she felt instantly awake, yet there was no sound which seemed to have woken her. The alarm clock was ticking noisily as usual, and showed the time to be half past two. Lindy lay for a moment, in the darkness, listening. Yes, there *was* a noise; a steady noise, like a wind blowing, but without the usual moans and rustles in the trees.

Slipping quietly out of bed, Lindy padded softly over to her window and pulled back one curtain. At first, she could not quite understand what it was outside. Then she realised. The snow, fine and plentiful now, was flying past her window horizontally. Tiny drifts had gathered thickly in the corners of her window panes, and she could not see the roofs or anything outside. She rubbed the misty condensation from the window, but it was no better; still, all she could see was the fine, driving snow. Lindy let the curtain drop and turned back towards her bed, where Pinky was curled in a tight, tabby ball.

"You're all right," Lindy told him. "You're nice and warm, but what about Gypsy?" Pinky's nose remained tucked under his tabby front paw, and his eyes stayed tightly shut. Lindy sighed. She did not blame Pinky for wanting to stay asleep on a night like this, but how was little Gypsy faring, out in the blizzard?

"I'm going to see her!" Lindy announced suddenly to her unconcerned cat. Her decision made, Lindy hurriedly began pulling on any warm clothing she could find. Over her pyjamas she pulled trousers, two sweaters and a pair of thick socks. She searched in the top drawer of her chest of drawers and found a torch. Then, taking her coat from the hook on her door, she opened the bedroom door quietly and crept down the passage towards the stairs.

CHAPTER TEN

A Christmas Star

The house was quiet, but all around Lindy could hear the gentle roar of the blizzard. It was a noise that she had never heard before and it sent a shiver of fear through her. As she crept down the stairs, lighting her way with the torch, she thought of all the wild animals out in the storm. But most of all, she wondered about her pony.

She made her way through the kitchen where the range, closed up for the night, clinked occasionally, like some big, warm animal, sighing in its sleep. In the scullery, Lindy thrust her feet resolutely into her wellington boots.

Now that she had arrived at the back door, Lindy hesitated. The world outside sounded somehow alien and sinister, as the blizzard roared. Then she thought again of Gypsy and she lifted the latch.

The yard which met Lindy's eyes was

not one that she was used to. Everywhere there was fine, driving snow, but through it Lindy could see a strangely softened world. There were no sharp edges. The cobbles were covered by a thick white blanket of snow that thickened into a snowdrift as it reached the wall, which seemed to have shrunk in height. The sheds sported thick white snow thatches.

The beam of Lindy's torch seemed tiny and insignificant as she shone it into the yard. Taking a deep breath, she stepped out cautiously. The snow reached more than halfway up her boots. Trying not to think that she was outside, on her own, in a blizzard in the middle of the night, Lindy closed the door behind her, put her head down against the driving snow, and made her way carefully in the direction of the orchard gate. Walking was slow, for she had to lift each foot up high before taking the next step. Reaching the gate, Lindy pushed the snow off the bars to find the latch. Using all her strength, she pushed open the gate, stopping every now and then to move some of the snow aside with her hands. Already, her fingers were cold and wet through her woollen gloves.

In the orchard at last, Lindy could feel

the frozen grass underneath the snow crunching beneath her feet as she high-stepped in the direction of the shed. The torchlight picked out the dark shapes of the apple trees, their gnarled branches etched in white. At last, the beam shone on the side of the shed. Lindy's heart quickened as the torchlight found Gypsy.

Gypsy stood with her back to the storm. Blown snow clung to her tail and hindquarters, and her head was lowered and faced into the shed. Lindy called to her and Gypsy turned her head sharply. She whinnied; a long, low grateful call that filled Lindy's heart with delight.

Still stepping high through the snow, Lindy talked to Gypsy as she neared her. Gypsy whinnied again, gently, and then lowered her head, looking again into the shed.

At last, Lindy reached the shed. She stopped, her hand on Gypsy's quarters. The snow was driving across the open side of the shed, but inside it was less cold and it was dry, and at last Lindy was able to walk without lifting her feet high at each step.

"Hullo, you lovely little pony," Lindy murmured, smoothing Gypsy's neck, which was still lowered. Gypsy seemed to be eating the hay which Lindy had left in the corner of the shed for her.

"So you decided you liked the hay, after all," Lindy said, "I told you it was Dad's—" She stopped, suddenly, unable for a few moments to believe her eyes.

Gypsy was not eating the hay. She was gently licking a tiny black foal which lay in the corner of the shed!

After Lindy had overcome the initial shock, she peered anxiously at the foal, which gazed back at her from big, dark eyes. It looked quite well, as did Gypsy, who was still busily licking it. As Lindy watched, fascinated, the foal began to struggle awkwardly to its feet, its spindly legs wobbling. Finally, it stood, swaying slightly, on all four legs. Lindy did not dare to take her eyes off it, in case it disappeared.

As the foal stumbled awkwardly towards its mother, Lindy thought she heard someone calling. She turned and stepped out of the shed, shining the torch's beam into the snow. Into the pool of light came Susan, bundled in scarves and wearing Dad's old sheepskin coat. Lindy stumbled through the snow to meet her.

"Lindy," Susan called, "thank goodness you're here. I was *so* worried."

"It's Gypsy," Lindy shouted above the noise of the blizzard, her voice shrill with excitement. "She's had a foal!"

Susan stopped, her eyes open wide. "She's had a . . . what?" she stammered.

"A foal!" Lindy shrieked, excitement overtaking her.

The amazed expression on Susan's face was replaced by a wide smile. She grasped hold of Lindy's hands. "But . . . that's wonderful," she said.

"Come and see," said Lindy, excitedly, pulling Susan towards the shed.

Together, they stumbled through the snow to the shed and stood, in silence, still hand in hand, watching Gypsy and her foal.

"I just can't believe it's true," Susan breathed at last, turning to look at Lindy, her eyes shining. "She was so thin – but I've heard of this sort of thing happening before; especially with first foals."

They smiled at each other – a smile of sharing. Susan put her arm round Lindy's shoulders as they both turned to look at the foal again.

"What a wonderful Christmas present she's given you," Susan murmured.

Then, suddenly, her voice was brisk. "But what *are* we thinking of, standing here. We must get Gypsy and her foal into a stable."

"But – won't Dad be cross? You said yourself that it's expensive keeping ponies in."

"Yes, I know," Susan replied, "But this is different, isn't it?" She smiled at Lindy, mischievously. "It'll be two against one," she said. "We'll overrule him! Besides," she added, "look what a wonderful bargain you've got – two ponies for the price of one!"

Before they closed the stable door, Susan and Lindy turned back for one last look at mother and son, comfortable, warm and away from the blizzard. Gypsy stood knee-deep in straw, munching contentedly at her hay, whilst the foal, curled sleepily in the corner, was nearly lost to sight in the straw.

"I wonder what story Gypsy could tell," Susan said. "I suppose we shall never know. But you know," she added, thoughtfully, "that foal looks quite a good one to me."

Lindy looked at her, curiously.

"My father used to breed Connemaras," Susan explained.

"So you know about ponies?"

"A bit," Susan admitted. "Enough, anyway, to know that your little foal is going to be quite a good-looker when he grows up."

"I love the white patch on his forehead," Lindy said.

"Yes. It seems like a good name for him, doesn't it – Star; especially since it's Christmas."

Lindy nodded. She thought of Mum and the first star. "Mum would have liked that name," she said, quietly.

Susan squeezed her hand. "I'm sure she would," she said, gently.

Leaving the blizzard outside, Lindy and Susan tumbled into the scullery. Susan shut out the night.

"Thank goodness," she said. "Now we can let our hands and feet thaw out."

"What hands and feet!" Lindy laughed. "I can't *feel* any!"

"I know!" Susan said, as they walked into the kitchen. "Hot chocolate – that should warm us up."

"Lovely," said Lindy. She shivered.

"And while you make it, I'll go and see if the curtain is over the front door – it seems draughty in here."

A large, heavy curtain was hung over the front door to help to keep out the draughts which were plentiful in the old farmhouse. Lindy found that the curtain was not quite across, so she tugged it into position and bent down to tuck in the ends to make sure that no draughts could creep underneath.

As she pulled at the thick material near the wall, her fingers touched something made of paper. Pulling at it, she found that a letter had become lodged in the broken end of the curtain's hem. Lindy found herself looking at an air-mail envelope addressed to Susan.

Thoughtfully, Lindy made her way back to the kitchen, where Susan was waiting for the milk to boil.

"That's better," Susan said, looking up. "I felt the draught disappear." She had opened the door of the range, and hot coals glowed cheerfully behind the metal bars.

"There, it's ready." Susan poured the hot milk into two mugs. "What have you got there?" she asked, handing a steaming mug to Lindy.

"I found it by the front door – it was caught up in the curtain." Lindy looked at her stepmother curiously, and added quietly, "Is this what you have been waiting for, Susan?"

Susan looked at Lindy, quickly. "How did you know?" she asked. Then she looked down at the letter, and happiness shone in her eyes. "Oh, Kim, so you *did* write," she said, softly, tearing open the envelope and reading, hungrily. At last, she put the letter down and smiled at Lindy. "So she hasn't forgotten me after all," she said, "and she may be coming to see me next year."

"But who is Kim?"

"Oh, of course. You don't know. Kim is my daughter. She lives in Canada, now, with her father. She's about your age – she looks a bit like your friend, Kate."

Now Lindy understood. She had known that Susan had been divorced about a year before she met Dad, but she had been so antagonistic and difficult about the marriage that she had never bothered to ask anything about Susan or her family.

"But why does Kim live with her father and not with you?" she asked.

"I was ill," said Susan. "That was

88

partly why we had the divorce. Peter – that's my first husband – he was always a restless type and he hated illness. We had grown apart, anyway. Our marriage never really worked, but we stayed together because of Kim – not a very sensible thing to have done, really, I suppose." Susan stopped for a moment and gazed thoughtfully into the fire, before continuing. "Then, when Peter decided to emigrate to Canada, and we agreed to get a divorce, we thought it a good idea for Kim to go with him. Of course, it was a terrible wrench, but at the time it seemed the right thing to do. There are so many opportunities in Canada. Peter and I agreed that Kim should decide for herself, when she was a little older, whether she wanted to live permanently in Canada or come back here and live with me." Susan smiled thoughtfully. "I *do* miss her, though – and I think maybe she sometimes misses having a mother around. You know that feeling, don't you, Lindy?" Susan added gently. She looked at Lindy. "We haven't really had a chance to talk before, have we?"

Lindy shook her head. "That was my fault," she admitted.

"No," said Susan. "We just needed

some time to get to know each other." She gazed into the fire, her letter forgotten in her lap. Then she turned again to Lindy. "We'll try from now on, shall we?" she said.

They smiled at each other and as they did, the kitchen door opened. Dad appeared in the doorway.

"Good heavens," he said. "I thought it must be Father Christmas in here! Whatever are you two doing?"

"Well, now," Susan said, slowly. "We've got something to tell you . . ."